FROG LEGS

Adapted by Lara Bergen
Based on the teleplay by Eric Weiner
Illustrated by Alisa Klayman-Grodsky

Based on the "Stanley" books created
by Griff with ticktock publishing, ltd.

Printed in the United States of America
First Edition
1 2 3 4 5 6 7 8 9 10

Library of Congress Catalog Card Number: 2003096533
ISBN: 0-7868-4556-2

What a beautiful day! Stanley thought when he woke up. He couldn't wait to do something fun.

"Dennis, wake up!" Stanley shouted to his pet goldfish. "C'mon! Let's go to the zoo! Or the pet shop! Or the dinosaur museum!"

But Dennis wasn't quite as eager as Stanley to get out of bed.

"Stanley," he moaned. "Can't I sleep just a little more?"

Just then, Stanley's dad came in, wearing swim trunks and goggles and carrying a towel.

"Guess where we're going?" he said to Stanley.

"The aquarium?" Stanley asked.

"Nope," said his dad. "We're going swimming! This summer you're ready to go swimming in the big pool!"

On the drive to the pool, Stanley's big brother, Lionel, was having fun listening to music, while Stanley was busy worrying. He was afraid of trying something so new. The big pool was just so—*gulp*—big.

"I've never been in the big pool before," Stanley whispered to Dennis.

"Well, Stanley," Dennis told him, "when you're afraid of something, the best thing to do is face your fears head-on."

"I was afraid you were going to say that," Stanley said with a sigh.

Stanley's friends, Mimi and Marci, were already playing in the big pool when he got there. They waved to him.

"Come swim with us!" they shouted.

"Go on, Stanley! Try it," Dennis urged.

Stanley put on his water wings and walked toward the pool. But the blue water looked *so* deep to Stanley. He knew he wasn't ready. Instead, Stanley waved back . . . and ran into the locker room.

"Well, so much for swimming in the big pool," said Dennis.

"You like swimming because you're a fish," Stanley said. "But I'm a kid, and I don't."

"That's because you haven't tried it,"
Dennis said. "There are quite a few animals
who like being on land and in water. They're
called *amphibians*. Frogs, for instance, are
amphibians."

Suddenly, Stanley started to smile.

"Dennis," he exclaimed, "you're a genius!"

If he could find out more about frogs,
maybe he could learn to like being on land
and in water, too!

But where could Stanley learn more about frogs?

Luckily, he had *The Great Big Book of Everything* with him!

Stanley pulled out the book and turned the pages. "A . . . B . . . C . . . D . . . E . . . F—Frogs!"

"Hey, look, Dennis," Stanley cried as he saw a picture of a fat green frog climbing out of a pond and onto a lily pad. "You were right! This frog's happy on land *and* in water."

Then Stanley and Dennis leaped into the book.

"Wow, look at her go!" Stanley exclaimed. "How does she jump so far?"

That's when Dennis explained that frogs have very strong legs. On land, they can jump twenty times the length of their own bodies!

Then
Stanley and
Dennis watched the
frog jump back into the
water.

"Her strong legs help her
swim, too. And see those webbed feet?"
Dennis asked Stanley as they watched their frog
friend swim across the pond. "That helps the frog
push her way through the water very fast!"

The next thing Dennis knew, he and Stanley were back in the locker room and Stanley was jumping up and down.

"I've decided to be a frog!" he declared. "Then I'll be able to jump really far, swim really fast, and like being on land and in the water! *Ribbit! Ribbit!*"

But Dennis reminded Stanley that there was just one little problem with this plan—Stanley was *not* a frog.

Just then, Stanley's dad came in to see what he was doing. "We're all waiting for you to come play in the pool," he told Stanley.

That's when Stanley noticed some flippers and goggles hanging on the wall. He imagined the flippers to be frog legs and the goggles to be big, bulging frog eyes.

"I've got an idea!" he cried. "Can I wear those in the pool?"

"Well, sure," his dad replied. "Why not?"

Stanley put the flippers and goggles on and began to hop around the locker room—just like a frog.

"I can do it!" he shouted. "I can go into the big pool. After all, what's a little water to . . . Stanley the Frog Boy!"

Minutes later, Stanley hopped out of the
locker room . . . straight into the big pool!
"He did it!" Stanley's dad shouted.
"Way to go!" Lionel cheered.
"Hooray!" cried Dennis.
"Oh, Stanley, I'm so proud of you,"
his mom said happily.

And for the rest of the day, Stanley swam around the big pool, playing with his friends, truly as happy in the water as on land.

That night, Stanley thought about his fun day, and all the things he had learned about frogs. They could swim so fast and jump so far, *and* they could live both in water and on land!

Still, Stanley was glad he was Stanley, and not really a frog boy. And he was glad he had a friend like Dennis.

"Guess what, Dennis?" he whispered as he turned off the light. "You're the best friend on land or water."

"Good night, Frog Boy Stanley," Dennis said with a grin.

DID YOU KNOW?

- A group of frogs is called an "army."
- Frogs don't drink water—they absorb the water they need through their skin.
- A frog's nose and eyes are on top of its head so it can still see and breathe even while it's swimming.
- Frogs have been on the earth since the time of the dinosaurs.

HELP STANLEY AND DENNIS GET TO THE OTHER SIDE OF THE POND.

START

FINISH

Special thanks to Eli Bryant-Cavazos, Senior Keeper, Herpetology, at The Baltimore Zoo, for help with the "Did You Know?" facts.